FREE THE WHALES

"...ntertaining and cleverly written... This is a fu ny, heart-warming tale that glancingly touches s(eral chords close to a child's heart. An u equivocal winner." *Scotland on Sunday*

" large-print chapter book which all children who a bsessive about articles of clothing will enjoy... A d of Free Willy III."
T es *Educational Supplement*

J ix is the son of actors Brian Rix and Elspet (*26* s well as being a writer, he's a TV director a ducer of shows such as *Faith in the Future*, *I* atrol and *Harry Hill*. His first children's b rizzly Tales for Gruesome Kids, was published i)0 and was the Smarties Book Prize (en's Choice. He has since written two other c ions of stories, *Ghostly Tales for Ghastly Kids* a earsome Tales for Fiendish Kids as well as the r *The Dreaded Lurgie* and *A. Stitch in Time*, and t ooks about a love-crazy boy, *Johnny Casanova* a *The Changing Face of Johnny Casanova*. l ied with two sons, he lives in south London.

Books by the same author

Grizzly Tales for Gruesome Kids
Ghostly Tales for Ghastly Kids
Fearsome Tales for Fiendish Kids
Johnny Casanova
The Changing Face of Johnny Casanova
The Dreaded Lurgie
A. Stitch in Time

JAMIE RIX

Illustrations by Mike Gordon

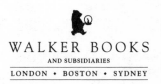

WALKER BOOKS
AND SUBSIDIARIES
LONDON • BOSTON • SYDNEY

For John and that T-shirt

First published 1997 by
Walker Books Ltd, 87 Vauxhall Walk
London SE11 5HJ

This edition published 1998

4 6 8 10 9 7 5 3

Text © 1997 Jamie Rix
Illustrations © 1997 Mike Gordon

This book has been typeset in Garamond.

Printed in Great Britain by Clays Ltd, St Ives plc

British Library Cataloguing in Publication Data
A catalogue record for this book
is available from the British Library.

ISBN 0-7445-5499-3

CONTENTS

CHAPTER ONE

Under normal circumstances, if a whale sits on your chest, you're dead. You're flattened flatter than a flat-ironed flat fish. So how come Alistair McAlistair had THREE whales sitting on his chest at the same time and lived to tell the tale?

Did he have a rubber body? Did he pump iron? Did he tie a thousand helium balloons to the whales' tails? Well, of course not!

The whales were printed on his favourite T-shirt. FREE THE WHALES screamed the bright red slogan splashed across his belly, while on his chest three cute killer whales squirted spouts of salty sea water into his armpits.

Alistair McAlistair loved his FREE THE WHALES T-shirt more than he loved marshmallows spread with marmalade, more than floppy, ploppy puppies with velvet pouffes for paws, more even than spaghetti bolognaise.

It fitted him just right. Not too big and not too small. Not too pinchy under the arms and not too long and lumpy for tucking into shorts. Not too tight around the neck, but not too baggy either (which was important, because baggy-necked T-shirts let the wasps in). Alistair McAlistair's T-shirt was like a second skin, only with whales tattooed on.

And like a second skin, Alistair McAlistair never took it off.

He wore it all day and every day;

for burpday parties,

BURP!

FREE THE

for backwards
bicycling,

for window
whistling,

for prawn
purchasing,

for hairy
hopscotch,

for school rule
fooling,

for seaside tripping
(to give the whales
a glimpse of home),

for Granny's salad
dressing making,

for tiger tickling,

for TV stewing,

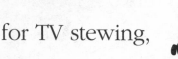

for insect
interrogating,

for laughing at lorries,

for nose-hole
moling,

for best   and for bed,

15

but never, not ever, no NEVER for
fishing, lest he accidentally give
offence to the whales and make
them disappear.
Because, for
Alistair
McAlistair, the
whales were
the thing! The
cotton was
comfortable,
but the
whales were
Alistair
McAlistair's
friends. He liked
their smiles.

CHAPTER TWO

One morning, while he was admiring his whales in the mirror, Alistair McAlistair decided to give them names.

"You're Willy, you're Wally and you're Walter," he said.

"And you're smelly," said his mother,
approaching Alistair McAlistair from
behind with a long, pair of wooden
pincers. "You've been wearing that T-
shirt for three months. It's time to take
it off."

But Alistair McAlistair wouldn't let her touch it. He turned himself into a tortoise, by curling up into a tight ball and hiding under a cardboard box.

"It's cruel," he sobbed. "Willy, Wally and Walter hate washing machines."

"They're just pictures," said his mother.

"And you're just horrid," blubbed Alistair McAlistair. "Whales are born to roam the open seas, not to be crammed inside a stuffy, old washing machine and spun round and round till they're sick."

So the T-shirt stayed on. Three
months later it was stiff with goo
and smelled like a vase of dead
flowers. No matter how many cans
of air freshener his mother bought,
the stink still lingered. She even
wore a clothes peg on her nose,
but the smell seeped through.

Eventually, it was so bad that she hatched a plot to steal the T-shirt while Alistair McAlistair was asleep.

That night, she crept into his bedroom and rolled him on to his side. Then she snapped on a pair of rubber gloves and gently started to peel the T-shirt off his back.

Unfortunately, as she tugged it over his head, the wicked whiff wafted up his nostrils and kick-started his brain. Alistair McAlistair sat up in bed and scowled. His mother innocently pretended she was checking his back for chicken-pox spots, but they both knew exactly what she'd been doing.

The next night she tried again, only this time she was more cunning. She stood out of sight behind the bedroom door and fished for the tangy T-shirt with a rod and line. But the hook snagged the duvet by mistake and when she reeled in her catch, the cover rose from the bed like a lumpy ghost, leaving Alistair McAlistair exposed to the sharp night air.

Cold toes made him wake with a start and cold toes foiled his mother's plan for the second night in a row.

By the third night, Alistair McAlistair had wised up. He installed a burglar alarm in his T-shirt, with heat sensitive pads that could detect even the featheriest of touches. When his mother slipped her sewing scissors up the armhole to cut the T-shirt in two, a socking great siren howled inside Alistair McAlistair's pillow. He jumped up and stared his mother in the eye.

"I wish you'd get the message," he said. "Me and the whales don't want to be parted."

At the end of a year, the T-shirt was so hard and crusty that Alistair McAlistair looked like an armadillo. It smelled worse than a scared skunk in a sauna and made the house hum like a two-storey stink bomb.

The niff billowed out of the chimney in gassy, green clouds and oozed through the brick walls on to the street. His neighbours moved out, local buses changed their routes and aliens from outer space altered their course to avoid planet Earth.

The Queen got a whiff of the T-shirt whilst sipping sweet sherry at a garden party, and told the Prime Minister to write to Alistair McAlistair's mother as a matter of supreme urgency.

Dear Alistair McAlistair's
Mother,

    Alistair McAlistair's foul
and funky FREE THE WHALES T-
shirt is burning a hole in the
ozone layer. Wash it Immediately
or I shall send in the army.

    Love

    The Prime Minister

CHAPTER THREE

Alistair McAlistair's mother sat
Alistair McAlistair down and
described the terrible weapons that
the army would use to destroy his
favourite T-shirt if he didn't let her
wash it.

"Flame throwers?" gasped Alistair
McAlistair. "You're not serious?"

His mother nodded. "And tanks," she added. "And stealth bombers."

Alistair McAlistair rushed upstairs to his bedroom and locked the door.

"I won't let them take you away," he cried to Willy, Wally and Walter, as an army helicopter dropped out of the sky and hovered outside his window.

"ALISTAIR McALISTAIR," boomed the voice of the pilot over the helicopter's loudspeaker.

Alistair McAlistair's mother was banging on the door.

Take off your T-Shirt and hand it to your Mother for washing. Do this **now** and no harm will come to you!

"Do as they say," she begged. "If the army takes your T-shirt by force, you'll never see the whales again."

"But I don't want to lose them," sobbed Alistair McAlistair.

"Then let me wash the T-shirt,"
pleaded his mother. "Slide it under
the door and I'll send the helicopter
away." Alistair McAlistair turned to
the mirror with tears in his eyes.
The whales, however, were still
smiling.

"I'm sorry," he sniffed, "but this is
for your own good." Then he
struggled out of his grime-stiffened
T-shirt and posted it under the door
into his mother's grateful hands.

CHAPTER FOUR

The washing machine sloshed and churned like a whirlpool. Alistair McAlistair sat on the kitchen floor and watched his favourite T-shirt tumble in and out of view.

He could see Willy, Wally and Walter diving in and out of the white-water waves, while the bright red slogan on the front of the T-shirt flashed intermittently past the thick glass door like a stuttering image in a magic lantern. FREE THE WHALES... FREE THE WHALES... FREE THE WHALES...

When the wash had
gone full cycle and
the machine had
gently purred to
a halt, Alistair
McAlistair's
mother clicked
open the
rubber-sealed
door and
removed the
T-shirt. It was
whiter than white.
It sparkled like a bank of freshly
fallen snow and smelled like
a sea of butter-kissed flowers in
a newly-mown meadow.

Sniff
Sniff

"There. Now that wasn't so hard, was it?" she said, as she flapped the wrinkles out of the T-shirt. Alistair McAlistair allowed himself a smile.

"Not hard at all," he agreed. "Can I put it back on now?"

"When it's dry," said his mother. turning the T-shirt over to smooth out the front. Alistair McAlistair caught his breath.

"Where are Willy, Wally and Walter?" he choked with horror. "Where are my whales?"

The front of the T-shirt was blank. The whales had washed off and in place of the original, bright red slogan was a new message, which read THE WHALES ARE FREE.

An emergency plumber was
called to dismantle the washing
machine in case Willy, Wally and
Walter were stuck inside, but he
found nothing.

"They've probably
been sucked
into the
drains," said
the plumber,
using his
expert
knowledge of
the sewage
system to solve
the mystery of
the missing

mammals.

"Then they're lost forever!" howled Alistair McAlistair.

"Oh, I shouldn't think so," said the plumber. "The drains lead directly into the River Thames."

CHAPTER FIVE

In a flash of blinding light all
became clear to Alistair McAlistair.
He stopped crying, jumped up off
the floor and bundled his mother
into the car. "Drive east!" he
ordered. "But why?" she asked, as
they swerved through the traffic.

"Because 'The Whales Are Free',"
grinned Alistair McAlistair, quoting
the T-shirt. "Don't you see? They're
not on my T-shirt, they're not in the
washing machine and they're not in
the drains. They're in the river
heading out to sea!"

The car clipped a concrete bollard and swerved across the oncoming traffic as Alistair McAlistair grabbed the steering wheel out of his mother's hand.

"The river's down there!" he shouted, redirecting the car towards the choppy, grey water.

"I know!" yelled his terrified  mother, whose eyes were popping out on stalks.

"Alistair, let go! That's a pavement!"

Too late! The wheels bumped up the kerb, sending three hubcaps spinning into the gutter and giving a puddle-bathing pigeon the shock of its life.

"Alistair, you're going to kill us!" But Alistair McAlistair wasn't listening. He had eyes only for the water.

"Can you see them?" he cried, as the car trundled along the pavement, nudging a sleeping fisherman into the river. "There! Mum, look! Over there! Stop!" As the car screeched to a halt, Alistair McAlistair leapt out. His little legs buckled as they hit the moving

pavement. He tumbled forward in a whirlwind of flying arms and legs and scrambled up the wall that ran along the riverbank.

"Willy, Wally, Walter!" he cried, waving to the three glistening, black humps that cut through the water like warmblooded submarines.

"They're alive!" he whooped, his heart bursting with joy. "I told you they would be."

"Haven't they grown!" said his mother. "Well of course they have," laughed Alistair McAlistair. "We've set them free!" A shiver of excitement ran down his spine like a fizzing sparkler.

Seeing the whales free gave him much more pleasure than having them printed on his T-Shirt had ever done. He turned back towards the river and gazed at his three beautiful friends. Their blow holes shot plumes of sparkling water high into the air as they swam towards the sea.

Suddenly his mother pointed
up-river and cried, "They're too big!
They're going to get stuck under
Tower Bridge." Alistair McAlistair
followed her gaze, and his heart
skipped a beat. His mouth went dry.

"Willy, Wally,
Walter!"
he croaked.
"Turn round!"
but the wind
whipped his
words into
the gathering
storm clouds
and the whales
kept swimming.

"We've got to help them," he urged his mother. "They'll die if we don't. Come on, run!" He grabbed his mother's hand and dragged her along the towpath towards the bridge. His lungs were bursting as he sprinted to the foot of the tower where the man who operated the bridge's lifting mechanism worked.

CHAPTER SIX

"There are whales coming up the Thames!" he shouted, as the bearded man poked his head out of a tiny top window. "Lift the bridge!" The man gasped with surprise as he spotted the three gleaming humps in the water. Ducks he was used to, but whales were unusual.

"There's not enough time," he bellowed.

Alistair McAlistair burst into tears.

"It's their only chance!" he begged, glancing nervously at the looping leviathans. The man in the tower knew this to be true. "Hold on tight, then," he hollered, breaking every rule in the book.

The ground under Alistair
McAlistair's feet started to slip away
as the bridge split down the middle.
The two halves opened up like a
snake's jaw and rose into the sky.

His mother screamed as she slid
down the bridge towards the water.

"Grab on to the safety rails!" cried
Alistair McAlistair, as he clung on
for dear life himself.

"Help!" screeched his mother.
"I can't hold on forever!"

She didn't have to. Willy, Wally
and Walter were now directly below
the bridge, their fins scraping
along the metal
struts which

underpinned the broken road.
Then with a rolling dive they glided
gracefully through the arch
and headed
downstream.

"Goodbye!" shouted Alistair McAlistair. This time the wind was kind to his words and carried them down to the water's edge where the three whales could hear them. They rolled over on to their backs and smiled up at the tiny figure dangling

off the yawning bridge. Alistair
McAlistair waved one arm for all it was
worth, and the cute killer whales
flapped their flippers in reply. Then
they were gone. With a flick of their
sleek tails they plunged into the depths
and swam towards the sea and
freedom.

When the bridge had been lowered and his mother had stopped screaming, Alistair McAlistair gave her a kiss.

"Can I have a new T-shirt now?" he asked. "Not with whales on," she said firmly. So they bought one with a picture of Tower Bridge on instead, because bridges, unlike whales, are happy to stay in one place all their lives.

MORE WALKER SPRINTERS
For You to Enjoy

☐ 0-7445-4739-3   *Posh Watson*
                    by Gillian Cross/Mike Gordon   £3.50

☐ 0-7445-5406-3   *The Perils of Lord Reggie Parrot*
                    by Martin Waddell/David Parkins   £3.50

☐ 0-7445-5483-7   *The Most Brilliant Trick Ever*
                    by Judy Allen/Scoular Anderson   £3.50

☐ 0-7445-5241-9   *Fort Biscuit*
                    by Lesley Howarth/Ann Kronheimer   £3.50

☐ 0-7445-5258-3   *Care of Henry*
                    by Anne Fine/Paul Howard   £3.50

☐ 0-7445-3666-9   *Beware the Killer Coat!*
                    by Susan Gates/Josip Lizatovic   £3.50

☐ 0-7445-5240-0   *Cup Final Kid*
                    by Martin Waddell/Jeff Cummins   £3.50

☐ 0-7445-5407-1   *Elena the Frog*
                    by Dyan Sheldon/Sue Heap   £3.50

Name   _____

Address _____

_____